Hogs Back Books

– a nose for a good book …

Published by
Hogs Back Books
34 Long Street, Devizes
Wiltshire
SN10 1NT
www.hogsbackbooks.com

Printed in Malta
ISBN: 978-1-907432-38-5
British Library Cataloguing-in-Publication Data.
A catalogue record for this book is available from the British Library.
1 3 5 4 2

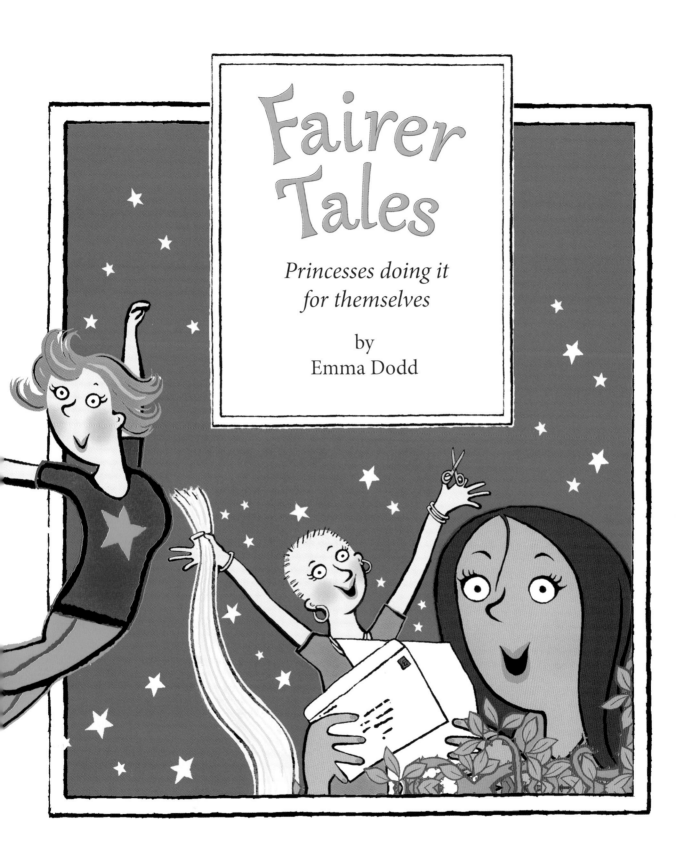

Fairer Tales

*Princesses doing it
for themselves*

by
Emma Dodd

In a land far, far away, three clever
young women are busy rewriting
their own fairy stories …

– Emma Dodd –

Dear Reader,

You may think that you already know the stories of Cinderella, Sleeping Beauty and Rapunzel, which you are about to read, but think again! You are in for a big surprise.

In these 'Fairer Tales' you'll read updated stories featuring modern heroines who are determined to do it for themselves and live happily ever after on their own terms. Perhaps you'll be inspired to follow suit.

What are your dreams? How will you get there? It's never too early to start planning your future, and remember anything is possible.

Best wishes,

Emma
x

Dear Grown-up,

Why, you may ask yourself, has HSBC UK helped create this book?

Our research shows that gender stereotyping within popular culture and within the stories we tell our children plays a key role in shaping attitudes and financial behaviours that last a lifetime. HSBC UK believes that if we can help turn this around, we will see children grow up to feel empowered and take control of their financial futures.

To help 'balance the books' we turned to award-winning children's author Emma Dodd. What you are about to read is the result – a new book that twists the traditional gender roles found in fairy tales so that the female characters no longer rely on Prince Charming to save them. Instead, it is their financial acumen that gets them through, setting a positive example for young girls and boys about how women can achieve goals on their own.

Talking about money with your children is a great way to build financial confidence, and we hope the following pages will help to lay the foundations for strong financial futures.

Happy reading!

Michelle Andrews
Michelle Andrews
Head of Banking and Propositions

Cinderella lives with her two grumpy sisters. Not only are they grumpy, they are lazy too.

Cinderella spends all her time clearing up after her sisters, cooking for them, and washing and ironing their clothes. No matter how hard she works, nothing is ever good enough.

To make matters worse, Cinderella's feet ache. She is on them all day and, with her toes crammed into uncomfortable, worn-out shoes, she can think about little else.

All day long, Cinderella dreams about comfortable shoes. But these are not any old shoes, they are the most stylish, most comfortable sports shoes ever worn.

Every evening, when all the housework is finished, Cinderella works quietly in her room, drawing page after page of beautiful sports shoes.

The grumpy sisters do not notice. They are too busy complaining and trying to impress the handsome Prince.

Then one day, an invitation to the Royal Ball arrives. The sisters are very excited, but none more so than Cinderella. Could this be her ticket out of here?

Cinderella looks down at her sore feet.

"How can I possibly dance in shoes like these?" she sighs, looking longingly at the shoe designs on her table.

Suddenly …

Cinderella's Fairy Godmother appears.

"You shall go to the Ball, Cinderella," she says, "but you don't need to marry a prince to get away from all this. You have everything you need for success and happiness right inside you!"

"Now you come to mention it," says Cinderella, "I have always wanted to design sports shoes."

With a wave of her magic wand, the Fairy Godmother changes a pumpkin into a sewing machine, the dish cloths into rolls of soft leather and a wooden spoon into a pair of sharp scissors.

Cinderella and her Fairy Godmother begin work on one of Cinderella's designs, and in no time they have made one of the most fabulous pairs of sports shoes imaginable.

Later that evening, Cinderella arrives at the Ball, proudly wearing her new shoes. They are admired by everyone; they are so springy, so bouncy, so stylish and so comfortable that she flies around the dance floor.

When the manager of Enchanted Forest Football Club sees her light-footed moves, he asks her to make football boots for his whole team. (The boots work like magic and the team wins every match of the season!)

Cinderella decides to open shops selling her footwear in every town and calls the shops "Glass Slipper Sports". She becomes world famous – everyone wants a pair of her amazing shoes.

Meanwhile, the Prince, who did not meet anyone he wanted to marry at the ball, rides off in search of a bride.

He has heard that there is a beautiful, sleeping princess, who has fallen under the spell of a bad fairy. She has been sleeping for nearly 100 years, and he hopes to break the bad fairy's spell by waking her with a kiss. (After all, isn't that what a fairytale prince is supposed to do?)

Sleeping Beauty's garden is overgrown because whilst she was sleeping there was nobody to mow the lawn or prune the hedges.

After fighting his way through the tangled bushes, the Prince finally arrives at the front door and rings the doorbell.

RING RING RING

RING RING RING

Sleeping Beauty wakes up from her deep sleep, puts on her slippers and dressing gown and goes to see what all the noise is about. But what is this she finds? There, on the doormat, lies an enormous pile of letters. A hundred years is a long time, and an awful lot of post has arrived!

Sleeping Beauty picks up a letter from the top of the pile. To her surprise, it is from her bank.

All the pocket money she put in the bank on her 18th birthday had been growing while she slept – just like the pile of letters, and she now has enough money saved up to do whatever she wants.

RING RING

Sleeping Beauty has forgotten all about the ringing at the front door. She opens it to find a young man standing there.

"I am Prince Charming!" he says. "I've come to wake you with a kiss and to take you for my bride."

"Thank you," says Sleeping Beauty, but I don't need a kiss because all your noisy ringing has already woken me up. And I'm certainly not going to marry you – we've only just met! Perhaps you could join me for a cup of tea instead? All that sleeping has made me very thirsty."

The Prince and Sleeping Beauty both enjoy a cup of tea, while she opens the rest of her post.

One of the letters is from her friend Rapunzel, who is trapped in a tower; held prisoner there by a wicked witch. The tower has no stairs and no doors, so Rapunzel is waiting to be rescued by a handsome prince.

"What can be taking him so long?" she thinks.

Rapunzel looks down at her long hair, which now almost touches the ground, and decides that she has had enough of all this waiting and will take matters into her own hands.

Taking out a pair of sewing scissors, Rapunzel cuts off her long hair …

… ties it firmly to the window frame and uses it as a rope to lower herself out of the window.

Free at last, Rapunzel visits the Wicked Witch to give her a piece of her mind and decides to make her an offer.

"I would like to buy the tower, please," says Rapunzel.

The Wicked Witch has grown tired of casting spells; there's no fun in it – young women are becoming too clever these days.

"Perhaps it would be better to sell the tower to Rapunzel," she thinks. "After all, it isn't much good to anyone. It doesn't have a staircase or even a door."

But Rapunzel has plans – she borrows money from the bank to turn the tower into three beautiful flats, adding doors and a staircase, as well as beautiful kitchens, bathrooms and bedrooms. She decides to live in the top one herself. It has magnificent views.

Rapunzel invites her friends Cinderella and Sleeping Beauty to live in the other two flats, and in return they give her money each month, which helps her to repay the money she has borrowed. After a while she receives enough money to buy more towers for more people to rent.

Rapunzel is now a free woman, who earns lots of money and is able to live well. She even has some spare money, which she can use to buy a share in Cinderella's new and exciting sports shoe business.

Cinderella, Sleeping Beauty and Rapunzel are all successful young women. They have used their brains, imagination and good sense to earn enough money to look after themselves without a prince charming in sight.

They decide to start a special club called The Fairy Godmothers, where they use their money to help other clever young people with brilliant ideas.

And guess what?